The Mystery At Lake Tahoe

By
Pamela Hillan & Penelope Dyan

Bellissima Publishing, LLC
Jamul, California
www.bellissimapublishing.com

Copyright © 2022 by Bellissima Publishing, LLC

All rights reserved. No part of this book may be reproduced or transmitted in any form or by any means, electronic or mechanical, including any photocopying, or recording, or by any information or storage retrieval system, without permission from the publisher and author.

ISBN 978-1-61477-575-1

First Edition

"Death has many secrets only found by looking closely."

About The Authors & The Book

Pamela Hillan and Penelope Dyan, lifelong friends who used to like to pretend they were in a Nancy Drew book when they were kids, are back again, all grown up (and then some); and they are still pretending! And this is exactly why the Jan and Jenny books continue to be written and why they began!

Penelope Dyan became a teacher, a published writer, a vocalist, and a mother and an attorney, while Pamela Hillan became a mother and a court reporter . . . and then finally, everything went back to what it was before all of that happened; and the Jan and Jenny books were born, beginning with their very first book in this series, "The Mystery On Burgundy Street".

It was their combined lifelong experiences, and their great desire to do good in this world, along with their love for the law, and their deep concern for humanity, that led to the creation of this latest book in the Jan and Jenny Mystery Series, and to each and every book in this series!

This is the twentieth book in this series; and Jan and Jenny are out to save the world once again, as they begin a new adventure that takes them on a chartered plane to Lake Tahoe, California with Jenny's family for what Jan and Jenny hope is a time to relax while Jenny's dad performs with his band. Meet Donnie and Drake and find out what they find in the burning forest that leads this foursome toward an exciting adventure, as they find out about the dark web, the deep web, and the surface web of the internet and the danger that lurks there.

Travel through the pages of this book with Jan and Jenny, and their newly found friends, Donnie and Drake; and never forget what is important in this world of ours that we call home.

The Mystery At Lake Tahoe

By
Pamela Hillan & Penelope Dyan

The Mystery At Lake Tahoe

CHAPTER ONE

ANOTHER TRIP

Summer was quickly approaching, and Jan and Jenny were trying to make plans for what they would hope would be an uneventful break in things. However, for Jan and Jenny, nothing was ever as simple as they would like it to be. Things just happened when they were around, wherever they were, wherever they went, wherever they even planned to go.

In the meantime, however, since imagining the worst never seemed to be a good idea, they sat on the twin beds in Jenny's bedroom, one of them on each adjoining bed; and Jan (pen and paper in hand) began their annual 'things to do' list.

"Maybe this summer we will finally get to relax," Jenny mused as Jan began to lay out some ideas for summer.

The Mystery At Lake Tahoe

"I think we should just hang out at the beach all summer," Jan told her. "We deserve it, and there's a non-stop bus we can catch one block over from your house on Waring Road."

Jenny smiled.

"There's also a bus that can take us to the movie theater on El Cajon Boulevard," Jenny added. "You know how much I love theater popcorn! And you can't get that anywhere else!"

Jan smiled.

"Let's definitely put that on our list!" she exclaimed.

"How about some miniature golf?" Jenny asked. "The bus can take us there as well . . . and there are always a lot of cute boys there."

"Done!" Jan exclaimed, as she added miniature golf to her list.

"I know! We can walk up to the tennis courts at the middle school and play some tennis . . . and . . ."

"And meet some cute boys!" Jan interjected, quickly adding tennis to the list.

Just then Jenny's Aunt Vi entered the room.

"Did you hear?" she asked.

"Hear what?" Jenny questioned back.

"We're all going to Lake Tahoe this summer! Your dad got a gig there for three whole weeks, and it's all expenses paid! And . . .

The Mystery At Lake Tahoe

Jan is also invited to go with us . . . and her parents already okayed everything!"

"Guess I'll have to make a new list!" Jan excitedly said, as she crumpled up the paper containing the things to do list she had been making. "It's back to the drawing board, Jenny!"

"Well, not exactly," Jenny told Jan as she retrieved the crumpled list from the floor where Jan had just excitedly thrown it. "It's only for three weeks, and three weeks does not an entire summer make!"

Jan laughed as she watched Jenny uncrumple the paper list she had just thrown on the floor.

"You're right!" she told Jenny. "I just got carried away. That's all."

Jenny uncrumpled the paper list she now held in her hands.

"Maybe we can just do a re-write," she told Jenny. "An addendum would seem proper."

Jan smiled.

"When do we leave?" she asked Jenny's Aunt Vi.

"The first weekend after school gets out," Jenny's Aunt Vi told her. "And I certainly hope you two can stay out of trouble for a change," she added.

"Who us?" Jenny asked. "When have we *ever* actually gotten into any trouble?"

"We *never* get into trouble," Jan added. "Trouble just finds us!"

"And then we have to take corrective action," Jenny said, as Jenny's Aunt Vi sat down next to her on Jenny's bed, took off her glasses, and began to clean the lenses using a tissue she removed from the pocket of an apron she was wearing.

No real response to that forthcoming, Jenny's Aunt Vi said, "Oh, and when your mom gets home from work, she's bringing home some Mexican food from Don Jose's. So, I'm here to get your orders!"

Jan and Jenny both smiled from ear to ear!

"Sounds good to me!" Jan told her. "And I'll have the usual," she added.

"Me too!" Jenny said.

"Okay. Then I will go into the kitchen and add two bean and cheese burritos with sauce, heated under the broiler to the list, with extra sides of fresh salsa!"

The girls smiled as Jenny's Aunt Vi got up and left the room. It looked like at least part of the summer was already in the mix. Now all they had to do was sit, wait, and see. Because with Jan and Jenny, the truth was . . . anything was possible, if not probable.

The Mystery At Lake Tahoe

CHAPTER TWO

TRIP PLANS IN THE WORKS

After enjoying the burritos Jenny's mother brought home from Don Jose's, Jan and Jenny decided to take a leisurely stroll to the local park and talk some more about the upcoming trip to Lake Tahoe. At Jan's behest, Jenny brought her laptop along so they could google Lake Tahoe attractions and decide what they thought would best suit them during their three weeks stay at Lake Tahoe.

Once they found a comfortable bench to sit on, after arriving at the nearby park, Jenny opened her laptop and typed, 'Lake Tahoe Summer Attractions'. Wow! Were they surprised at what popped up, 'The Ten Best Things To Do At Lake Tahoe'.

Jenny began reading the list to Jan, who was by this time sipping on one of the bottles of water the girls had brought along with them for each of them to drink.

The Mystery At Lake Tahoe

"Check this out, Jan!" Jenny exclaimed. "We sure won't be bored with all this stuff to do! There's a tour of the lake and waterfalls, for one. I didn't even know they had waterfalls, did you?"

"That's so cool," Jan exclaimed in return. "Nope. I didn't know that either. What else is there on that list, Jenny?"

"Well," Jenny began, "they have a small group photography half-day tour. And you know I love to take pictures!"

"Yes, Jenny," Jan replied rather impatiently. "We *all* know that. *And* you are great at it, too!" Jan added with a bit more enthusiasm. "That might be fun. What else is there to do?"

"There's a two-hour sailing cruise, and a day trip to Yosemite that's sounds really awesome!" Jenny added, getting more excited by the minute as she continued to read down the 'things to do' list.

"Wow," Jan squealed with excitement. "I hear Yosemite is fabulous! I'd love to do that!"

"Yeah, me too," Jenny sighed. "But that's a six-hour trip."

"That's okay, Jenny! We can do it!" Jan told her. "After all, we *do* have three whole weeks to fill!"

"Very true, Jan," Jenny answered absentmindedly, as she continued to peruse the list before her. "Oh, look!" she then quickly added, "there's a 'Wild West Day Trip' from Lake Tahoe to Virginia City, an old mining town, on a train! That sounds really cool, too!"

The Mystery At Lake Tahoe

"It all sounds like fun, for sure, Jenny" Jan said excitedly, as she began to imagine all the fun the activities would provide for the two of them. "I do *hope* we don't have to drag your brother and sister along, though."

Jenny grimaced, as she commented, "Oh, Jan. You just had to burst my bubble by bringing that up, didn't you?"

Jan sheepishly replied, "Sorry." And then, attempting to change the subject, she added, "So, what should we do first?"

Jenny, still scrolling down the long list provided by the website, scratched her head.

"I don't know! There's so much to choose from that I just don't know."

"I know," Jan interrupted, "let's do them all at once, on the very first day, that is!"

"I don't think that's exactly possible, Jan. There's not enough hours in the day to do that!"

And then both girls burst out in laughter, thinking about how much fun that really would be . . . if only a day had more than 24 hours in it! Of course, without any sleep, they would get really tired. What would they *really* end up doing? Once again, only time would tell. And right now, time simply was *not* telling! And the future, itself, was most certainly a mystery.

CHAPTER THREE

THE BEST LAID PLANS

"The best laid plans of mice and men often go awry, no matter how hard a person (or a mouse) can plan, no matter how hard (a person or a mouse) may try," Jenny surmised aloud, as the girls continued sitting on the park bench.

"What are you talking about now?" Jan asked, shaking her head in confusion.

"Oh, that's just my version of a poem by Scottish poet, Robert Burns, 'To a Mouse, on Turning Her Up in Her Nest With the Plough', written in 1785." Jenny said, offhandedly.

"And you know that how?"

"Oh, it just popped up on my laptop, and so I paraphrased it because it seemed to fit the moment."

"You are so weird, Jenny!"

The Mystery At Lake Tahoe

"And so, I have been told, Jan!" Jenny replied, to which the girls began to laugh.

"Let's just hope our nest isn't turned up by a plough," Jan laughed.

"It does seem like no matter how hard we may try, things never seem to go as planned."

"Maybe this time things will be different, Jenny. What could possibly go *wrong* on *this* trip?"

"I think we need to look at this in perspective," Jenny quickly added, as she thought about what she had just said. "I don't think things really go wrong when they turn out so right!" Jenny suddenly exclaimed, as though she was having an epiphany.

"I agree!" Jan told her. "Besides, whatever will be will be!"

"And the future's not ours to see!" Jenny quickly interjected, to which she added, "Isn't that a song?"

"Yup!" Jan told her. "And I think it should be our mantra!"

And then the girls began to sing! After all, wasn't all of life contained in poetry and song? It seemed that way to Jenny, even if Jan didn't always agree. Jenny surmised that it probably had something to do with her dad being a musician. It was how Jenny had looked at life from the time she sat in her highchair while her dad played 'Twinkle, Twinkle Little Star' on his trumpet for her during her 2 AM feeding, after her father had gotten home from work. It seemed that for Jenny, music was more than a scrambled bunch of notes. For Jenny, music was all a part of a great pattern of life, a pattern of life that has yet to unfold. And in Jan's heart, she also knew this was true. And this is why Jan and Jenny sang.

And so, they sang in two-part harmony as they walked back to Jenny's house. And even Jan, with all her planning, knew that some things in life just *couldn't* be planned. And she also knew that surprise was *always* a part of the plan, even if surprise couldn't possibly *be* planned.

The Mystery At Lake Tahoe

CHAPTER FOUR

HOW TIME FLIES!

The days passed quickly; and before they knew it, Jan and Jenny were in packing mode and ready to board another plane for their Lake Tahoe destination! And since Jenny's dad had a gig playing his trumpet at one of the big hotels at Lake Tahoe on the South Shore, the whole family, including Aunt Vi, brother John, and sister Chrissy were all included, along with Jenny's mom and dad, of course, and the ever-adventuresome duo, Jan and Jenny.

The whole family had been pre-booked in the Presidential Suite at the fabulous Harvey's Resort, Spa, and Casino! It was a sight to behold! The hotel was located lakefront, with fabulous views in every direction.

Being a small-time, big town celebrity had its advantages, it seemed. But for Jenny's dad it was never about things. It was always about the music!

The Mystery At Lake Tahoe

Jan and Jenny had made a list of places of interest they wanted to explore, knowing (of course) that they would need approval beforehand from Jenny's parents prior to finalizing any of their plans. However, since the girls were getting older into their teen years, they were allowed to be on their own quite a bit now (if it seemed safe). On this trip it was already decided that Jenny's Aunt Vi would chaperone John and Christine when Jenny's mom wasn't tagging along with them, and that the girls would be given more of a free rein. Jenny's dad would be busy with his band, since it was (after all) June, the busiest time of the resort's summer season. And his days would be filled with rehearsals and the like.

Once again, they were boarding a chartered plane to take them to their destination, only this time the plane was much nicer, newer, and quite large, compared to their last charter. So, everyone felt much safer on *this* plane. And besides that, it was only a short flight, basically just up the California coast.

The flight was pleasant, with no mishaps, which was a huge relief to everyone, after the terrible experience they'd had on their *last* chartered plane with Jenny's dad and his band on the way to Niagara Falls. (However, that was another story . . . and another time.) Even Jenny's mother (who hated to fly anywhere) remained calm.

The Mystery At Lake Tahoe

When the plane landed, a shuttle picked everyone up at the terminal and drove them straight to Harvey's, a world-renowned destination on the South Shore.

Jenny and Jan stepped out of the shuttle and gazed wide-eyed at the beautiful hotel.

"I can't believe we all get to stay in the Presidential Suite, Jenny. Can you?" Jan gasped, to which Jenny made no comment, as they all anxiously waited for the courier to retrieve their luggage and take them up in a beautiful private glass elevator to their living quarters.

"I feel like a rock star, Jenny! This is the greatest! Just look at this hotel! This is the most amazing hotel I've ever seen!" Jan exclaimed, grinning from ear to ear.

As they all walked by a brochure stand as they followed the courier through the huge hotel lobby, Jenny grabbed a brochure that caught her eye.

Once the whole family was together and through the lobby, taking more than one elevator trip up the private glass elevator to get the entire family (plus Jan) up to the Presidential Suite, they selected their individual accommodations as they wandered through the suite's spacious surroundings.

Nearly the entire suite was framed by floor to ceiling glass windows with glorious views everywhere they looked! They were twenty stories up into the sky! And . . . that made the view from every angle of the floor to ceiling windowed suite even more glorious! Jan and Jenny agreed it was the most majestic view they had ever seen!

Jenny pulled out the brochure she'd grabbed from the downstairs lobby and exclaimed excitedly as she pointed at the brochure, "Hey, Jan! Look at this! I think this should be our next destination! It's a 2.4-mile gondola ride right up into the 'Heavenly Mountains' to a 14,000-foot observation deck. Doesn't that sound awesome?"

"I suppose so," Jan said, as she sank down into a comfortable armchair in the room they had chosen and stared out their floor to ceiling window, and as she took the brochure from Jenny's hand and examined it more closely.

"Well? What do you think?" Jenny asked.

"I think we should do this ASAP!" Jan told Jenny, noting the activity began from just a short walk down the street.

And so . . . it was settled! And . . . it looked like the girls had their first day at Lake Tahoe planned! All they had to do now was clear it with Jenny's mom and dad!

The Mystery At Lake Tahoe

CHAPTER FIVE

THE OKAY!

The okay was a simple thing; and that night, after dinner, Jan and Jenny crawled into bed and slept soundly dreaming all night about the fun they had in store for them first thing in the morning . . . right after breakfast, that is! You see, Jenny's mother insisted that the family have breakfast all together as a family event, of sorts; because it was so seldom they even got to *have* breakfast together with Jenny's father, due to the fact his job as a band leader/trumpet player required him to work into the wee hours of the morning. So, breakfast for Jenny's dad usually came sometime in the afternoon when Jenny's mom was off to work, and Jenny and her sister and brother were off at school.

"I don't care much for breakfast, as you well know," Jenny told Jan, as they all headed down in the private elevator, two at a time, down to the main lobby first, and then over to the downstairs dining room for the advertised 'all-you-can-eat' breakfast buffet. "But I do love eggs benedict," she added, as Jenny's dad arranged for a table; and then they headed toward the buffet table.

"You're in luck!" Jan exclaimed, as she pointed to the posted menu on the wall behind the buffet table that said, 'eggs benedict at your request'. "It appears you can get your eggs any way you want them," Jan quipped with a giggle. "You're in luck, Jenny!"

Jenny smiled, as she and Jan followed the rest of Jenny's family ahead of them, ordering their breakfasts from the chefs who stood behind the glass protected counter.

"I want pancakes," Christine said. "I hate eggs!"

"I'll have some of everything on the menu," Jenny's brother, John, mumbled.

Jenny smiled, because she knew what her brother, John, had just said was more than likely what he wanted. . . some of 'everything'.

As they all went through the breakfast line and made their orders, Jan happened to notice that Jenny's brother really did seem to be getting a little bit of everything on the menu on his plate.

"I'm going to be a chef someday," John told Jan, with a smile. "I love to eat, and I love to cook," he added, as they headed back to their table where Jenny's mom, her Aunt Vi and Chris and Jenny's dad were already seated.

The Mystery At Lake Tahoe

"Your brother is very talkative today," Jan told Jenny, as they sat down at the table.

Jenny's dad held up his glass of orange juice.

"Saluti!" he said, with a smile. "Eat well! Eat heartily! Be strong!" he added.

Everyone at the table raised their juice glasses and responded, "Saluti!" as was the Italian custom, Jenny's dad being first generation American.

"I hope the waitresses and waiters don't think we are being too raucous," Jenny's mother said, as a waitress filled her turned up coffee cup.

"Not at all," the waitress told her. "We find your entire family quite delightful."

Hearing this, Jan and Jenny giggled.

"Let's hope she still feels that way by the end of our three week stay," Jenny said. And then she added, "By the way, these eggs benedict are really delicious!"

"So are my blueberry waffles, Jenny," Jan said.

"And my pancakes are really good too!" Christine chimed into the conversation, uninvited.

"Now tell me again what you two girls are planning for today," Jenny's dad said, looking straight at Jenny. "And promise me you two won't get into any trouble," he added with a note of skepticism.

Jenny lowered her eyes.

"We're going on a simple gondola ride to an observation tower," she told her father. "And Jan and I never go looking for trouble," she sheepishly added.

And while that was true, Jenny's dad gave Jenny that knowing look of his; and he simply said with a sigh, "I know . . . I know . . ." and then he returned to his meal.

After all, it was a simple tourist thing they were doing, so what could possibly happen?

"Do you think we could go water skiing tomorrow?" Jan asked Jenny.

"I'll ask my dad later," Jenny said. "Right now, we should probably take things one day at a time."

And as to that, Jan wholeheartedly agreed.

The Mystery At Lake Tahoe

CHAPTER SIX

FIRST THINGS FIRST!

After the family (and Jan) finished eating breakfast, Jenny suggested to Jan that the two of them go over to the concierge desk to check and see the availability for the gondola adventure that day. Jan agreed that it would be the smart thing to do, so off the two girls went to see *if* they could ride the gondola, and when. The rest of the family were scheduled for a miniature golf session at a close by location.

As it turned out, Jan and Jenny *were* able to get tickets for the gondola, as well as for the Tamarack Express chairlift (once they reached the top of the mountain) which they were told offered the best views of the entire area. The combination tickets meant that this was going to be a great day for an even greater experience than merely riding on the gondola! And to top it off, the concierge told the girls whatever they wanted to do during their stay would be comped! (It appeared that Jenny's dad, being a headliner, had its privileges!)

The girls were beside themselves hearing this! They could hardly wait to begin their three weeks of good old-fashioned fun!

The concierge then told the girls the hotel minivan would shuttle them the short way to the gondola (eliminating their need to walk to the gondola) and that the gondola held eight people at a time, so they should not be surprised if they weren't alone on the ride. They were also told that if and when they took the *extended ride* on the chairlift, there were lots of hiking trails, from beginner to expert, of which they could take advantage, and that they should be careful to dress appropriately if they intended to hike the mountainous, rocky trails.

Jenny signed for the tickets and took them in hand, no reservations necessary . . . simply show up and get in line, first come first serve.

"Don't worry," the concierge told the girls, "this time of day you won't find too many people in line."

As they went back up to their room to change into some proper hiking clothes, Jenny with a somewhat worried, furrowed brow said, "Boy, Jan, this might turn out to be an all-day experience. I sure hope we are up for it! I mean, it is *only* our *first* day."

"You're right, Jenny!" Jan exclaimed, realizing Jenny had made a very good point. "Maybe we should make this a two-part type of thing. The brochure you picked up in the lobby when we got here yesterday did *say* we could get our hands stamped if we wanted to come back later."

Jenny, not being the active, physical type was relieved.

"That sounds like a plan," she told Jan thoughtfully. "I just don't want the two of us to get worn out on the very first day out and about when we have a whole three weeks to enjoy this vacation."

"I hear you," Jan replied. "Let's just play it by ear."

And so, that's what they decided to do, play it by ear. And they took the private elevator back up to the presidential suite, ran to their room, threw open their suitcases, took out their hiking clothes and . . . dressed appropriately for the day!

"We really should probably unpack this stuff," Jan said, as she smoothed out her flannel shirt before putting it on, and then she put it on and donned her jeans and hiking boots.

"Well, at least . . . thanks to you, we brought the right clothes for this trip," Jenny laughed, in reference to Jan's planning for every possible occurrence and packing accordingly. "I was planning to just sunbathe by the swimming pool."

Jan smiled.

And then, after they were both fully and appropriately clothed for the day, having left nothing to chance, Jan grabbed a pair of

The Mystery At Lake Tahoe

binoculars she had packed in her suitcase, they donned their backpacks (after filling them with water and snacks from the suite's full-sized refrigerator) and they headed back down to the lobby in their private elevator, walked through the lobby, and went straight to the front doors of the hotel where the doorman called the minivan for them. The girls were ready for their first adventure!

And for Jan and Jenny, adventure was merely a part of life, and they were prepared for anything and everything!

CHAPTER SEVEN

Up, Up And Away!

As it turned out, there were only two other riders in the gondola that morning, Donnie and Drake. And as it *also* turned out, they were now heading to work, because they ran the chairlift on the extended ride as well as the gondola!

Jan gave Jenny a rather wry smile as they took their places in the gondola and the gondola headed up to the mountaintop.

Suddenly, the wind began to blow; and the gondola began to rock erratically back and forth.

"I'm scared," Jenny said, as she grasped the side of the open gondola next to where she sat.

Jan smirked.

"We'll be okay," she told Jenny. "We're always okay. We've seen worse."

The Mystery At Lake Tahoe

"I agree," the young man named Donnie said, interrupting Jan to offer a reassuring moment. "Everything will be just fine."

And after that, introductions were made.

"I'm Donnie, and this guy here is Drake. We run the extended chairlifts, if you happen to be doing that today."

"I'm Jan, and this is Jenny," Jan said nodding her head in the direction of Jenny, who happened to be sitting right next to her.

"Jan and Jenny?" Donnie asked . . . and then paused. "You don't happen to be *that* Jan and Jenny, do you?"

"Why? What have you heard?" Jenny interjected, still holding on to the side of the gondola as it continued to rock back and forth in the wind, chugging and jerking up to the mountain's top, much slower than before the winds had begun.

"Oh, not much," Donnie said, with admiration in his voice. "But if you *are* that Jan and Jenny, then I'm impressed."

Jan and Jenny both shrugged their shoulders and said nothing more, both preferring to travel incognito, which was becoming much more difficult as their reputations preceded them.

"Is this dangerous?" Jenny asked, directing her question to the quiet, conservative looking Drake.

"He's not as harmless as he appears," Donnie told Jenny.

"Neither is Jenny," Jan quipped back.

Then they all laughed, and Donnie explained that these things often happened when the winds started, and to date there had not been a single gondola mishap.

"I guess you should know," Jan said, with a wink. "You did say you two ran the extended chairlifts, after all."

Jenny sighed, and shook her head at Jan. She guessed Jan couldn't help her flirting. These two guys really were kind of cute. But it didn't seem like this was either the time or the place. And Jenny was becoming more concerned with every chug and jerking motion the gondola made!

And then it happened. The gondola stopped halfway up the mountain in midair.

Jan's eyes widened.

"Should we be concerned *now?*" Jenny asked, as Jan took the binoculars out from her backpack that she had placed at her feet.

"The girl comes prepared," Drake said.

"She always does!" Jenny exclaimed, as Jan put the binoculars up to her face, and began perusing the situation below them.

The young men just sat in silence. Apparently, this was a first-time occurrence for them; and they were close to being at their wits end.

"I'm sure the issue will be corrected shortly," Donnie said unconvincingly.

The Mystery At Lake Tahoe

And then Jan saw something. And she couldn't believe what she saw!

"What is it, Jan? What is it?" Jenny implored of Jan.

"Take a look!" Jan said, handing Jenny the binoculars. "Just look down there and to your right!"

Jenny took the binoculars in hand and did as she was told.

"Do you see it?" Jan asked. "Do you see it, Jenny?"

And Jenny saw what Jan saw. Vultures! There were vultures down there! And there was more than just one!

"I see them," Jenny said. "I see them, Jan," she repeated. "There are vultures down there! And it is *not* good!"

"They're probably just feasting on a deer's carcass," Donnie told Jenny.

Jan shook her head in the negative.

"That's no deer carcass, Donnie," Jenny said, as she handed him the binoculars. "Take a look and see," she added.

And so, just as the gondola headed up the mountain once again, Donnie saw what the girls had seen. And he handed the binoculars to Drake, and then Drake also saw what the girls had seen.

The vultures were most heartily feasting on the remains of what remained of a *human body.*

And the wind continued to blow.

The Mystery At Lake Tahoe

CHAPTER EIGHT

THE OBSERVATION DECKS

"We are almost at the halfway point observation deck. Once we are there, I'll call in that sighting of the body. I'm sure the Rangers will be on it right away. From time to time, we do have people getting lost on trails, especially if they are alone. It is always safer to travel with a companion, as I'm sure you girls already know," Donnie explained, as the gondola continued climbing.

"Wow! This trip hasn't even gotten started, and we are already finding dead bodies!" Jenny exclaimed, as they gated the gondola, ignoring the spectacular views beneath them as they sat in the gondola waiting to disembark.

What the girls had seen had left them a bit shaken, despite Donnie's words.

The Mystery At Lake Tahoe

"You know, it is possible that body was from a ski accident this past winter. Sometimes people are never found until the snow finally melts during our short summer season," Drake said by way of further explanation.

Both Jan and Jenny were skeptical.

"In any event," Drake continued, "whoever that poor person was (or is) at least *maybe* a family will have closure once the remains are recovered."

"Maybe no one knows that person is even missing," Jenny interjected wryly, much to Donnie's dismay, and to which (at that point) Donnie attempted to change the subject.

"Okay, gang! Let's step onto the platform here and enjoy some beautiful views!" Donnie said, attempting in vain to direct the group away from any further discussion about what they had just seen.

After the gondola was securely locked onto the platform by a special mechanism, Jan and Jenny had no fear of walking across the steel plate onto the observation deck. Once there, Jan and Jenny just stood there in amazement, gazing at the majestic views all around them, for a moment forgetting the terror they had just seen. The lake was glistening like diamonds from the sun's reflection. A pair of bald eagles soared above the trees, their wing spans enormous. And to Jan, they looked almost like glider planes, beautiful to behold.

The Mystery At Lake Tahoe

Jenny had the binoculars and was looking through them to the north. She thought she saw something.

"Is it my imagination, guys, or do I see smoke way over there in that big area of trees, just to the north?"

"Let me take a look, Jenny," Drake told her. "We're pretty high up here. It could just be some low clouds. Sometimes dark rain clouds look just like smoke."

Jenny turned to look in the opposite direction.

"I hope you're right about that," Jenny told him.

Since they had only reached the initial observation deck, Donnie suggested they should get back in the gondola and continue up the mountain, because there was still a whole lot left to do on the tour.

And so, without further discussion, they re-boarded the gondola once more and continued on to the top of the mountain, where there was an additional chairlift ride, if they were interested.

Jenny began to get a little short of breath due to the high elevation, which was a reasonable reaction. After all, they were now in excess of 10,000 feet!

"I feel like I might need oxygen," Jennie told Donnie. "It's getting hard for me to breathe."

"Breathe low and slow," Donnie told her. "Your respiratory system will adjust to the elevation soon."

"If you say so," Jenny replied as she took Donnie's advice and tried to do as he had said.

Jan began to worry about Jenny. She sat close to her on the bench inside the gondola, and she tried to calm her down. They were almost to the top of the mountain, and Jan hoped that once they were on solid ground Jenny would feel better.

But Jenny was having great difficulty calming down, and she couldn't stop thinking about what they had seen.

CHAPTER NINE

WHAT'S NEXT?

Jenny was beside herself. Anxiety was getting the best of her. She began to panic.

"I can't help it," Jenny said, as her hands began to shake. "This was supposed to be a time to relax. Why in the world does this stuff keep happening to us?"

Jan took Jenny by the hand and said, "Jenny, it's just who we are. This is what we were meant to do and who we were meant to be."

Then Jenny looked at Donnie and said, "Donnie, we have to locate that body and find out what happened to that person. I can't stand it any longer!"

"Is it possible to get down to where we saw the body?" Jan asked.

"I told you that it is probably nothing," Donnie told her.

"Was or is anyone missing?" Jan implored of him. "Is there any way we can find out? Can we check with missing persons or something? Who knows about this stuff, anyway?"

"Whoa! Hold your horses, Jan," Donnie said, almost laughing. "One question at a time is all I can take. I have a very short attention span."

It was at that point that Jan began to get angry.

"Look!" she said. "I don't know how you're used to doing things up here in Tahoe, but this is the real world. And Jenny and I aren't used to just sitting around and doing nothing when we perceive danger at hand. Reverse this thing and reverse it now!" Jan demanded.

At hearing those words, Jenny began to calm down, and the panic inside of her began to subside.

"You go girl!" she told Jan with a smile. And then looking at Donnie and Drake, she said, "I strongly suggest that you do exactly as Jan said, and that you do it right now!"

Donnie's eyes widened.

"We can't exactly go in reverse; but when we get to the top, we can go down," Donnie conceded.

"Then make it so!" Jenny told him. "And contact the local police authorities while you are at it!" Jenny further demanded.

Drake smiled at Jenny.

The Mystery At Lake Tahoe

"You girls certainly have spunk!" he said.

"And that just proves my point!" Donnie added.

"And what point is that?" Jan asked.

"It proves my point that you two girls are most certainly *that* Jan and Jenny!" Donnie quipped.

"Yes, we are!" Jan replied emphatically. "And don't you *ever* forget that!"

And so, the mystery began to unfold. Who was the corpse they had seen from the gondola? And what secrets had the corpse taken with it to its death?

Jan and Jenny would find out, because secrets always showed their ugly heads to Jan and Jenny when evil was afloat.

And then they saw the flames.

"So much for saying I saw dark clouds!" Jenny exclaimed. That's not rain! That's fire! And where there's smoke, there's *always* fire!"

And why was there fire now? That was the question.

"Do you suppose that the fire and that the body we saw are connected?" Jan asked Donnie.

Donnie said nothing.

"I'll bet you dollars to donuts the two things are connected!" Jenny emphatically added.

And then a humbled Donnie and Drake had to admit that Jenny might just be right! After all, they were *that* Jan and Jenny!

33

CHAPTER TEN

THE DESCENT

Donnie wasn't about to listen to anymore ranting by either of the girls, especially not opinionated Jenny!

"Okay, girls," he told them, giving in to Jenny's demand. "Get comfortable on the gondola bench! We're going back down the mountain!"

As the gondola started its descent, it began swaying violently back and forth in the wind again. Drake and Donnie were concerned, but they didn't want to scare the girls. After another hundred feet down the cable line, there was a loud screech.

Jenny looked at Donnie, as he was operating the gondola, and with her lips quivering she timidly asked, "What was that noise?"

Jenny did not want to further raise Donnie's ire.

"Just relax, Jenny. I have a handle on it." Donnie reassured her with a bit of disdain in his voice. "The winds are just picking up again. That's all. It's not that unusual."

The words were barely out of Donnie's mouth, when the gondola began to sway even more violently back and forth, almost to the point that the girls thought they might fall out of it.

"What's happening? This wind is terrible!" Jan screamed.

Donnie directed them to use the attached harnesses in the gondola for extra protection. Then he released the brake he had momentarily set at stop for a moment, hoping the wind would calm down. It didn't.

The gondola moved a few more feet. And suddenly, a huge spark flared on the cable line, and the gondola came to an abrupt stop.

Donnie *knew* what needed to be done, but he was reluctant to break the news to the others.

"Please tell me we aren't stuck up here dangling in midair!" Jenny yelled to Donnie over the howling wind.

"I'm afraid we have to climb down from here using the emergency fire ladder!" Donnie yelled back. "There's more than enough length on the rope ladder to get to the ground from here! I'm afraid we can't stay here any longer, because the cable system has frozen for some reason; and right now, this is our only recourse!"

Jan was uncharacteristically nervous. It looked like a long way down to the ground!

"Don't be nervous, Jan," Jenny told her. "It looks like there's lots of fluffy grass to land on, so we'll be okay. We always are!"

But then Jenny started hyperventilating. She didn't much care for heights in the first place, and now she was dangling in midair!

Donnie handed Jenny a portable can of oxygen that was part of an emergency kit on the gondola.

"Here, Jenny," he told her. "Take a couple of breaths of this. It should calm you down. We are going to be okay. I promise."

Jenny grabbed the oxygen face cup, put it up to her face, and took a deep breath. Donnie was right. It helped.

Jan, gaining her composure, turned back into her 'take charge' self.

"Okay," she said. "Let's do this! I can smell the smoke getting stronger from the fire. We should move fast."

Donnie threw the rope ladder over the side of the gondola. It extended *almost* all the way to the ground.

"It's only a few feet short," Donnie told the others. "It doesn't look like there are any sharp rocks or other obstacles down there that would interfere with our descent to ground," he added, as he turned to Jan. "Come here, Jan," he said. "I'll hold onto you, and we can tandem down together. Drake and Jenny can do the same.

Don't forget the backpacks," he added. "And bring the emergency kit, Drake! Put it in your backpack."

And then they climbed over the side of the gondola, Donnie first, grabbing Jan and holding onto her as they descended the ladder, backpacks in place on their backs. The wind had subsided a bit, so it wasn't as difficult climbing down as it would have been earlier.

When Donnie and Jan reached the end of the ladder, they leapt to the ground. Jan landed on top of Donnie . . . but neither of them was hurt.

Then Drake and Jenny came down the rope ladder just as easily and as safely! (The only difference was that Jenny managed to land a few feet away from Drake and not right on top of him.)

"What a relief!" Jan exclaimed, once they were all safe on solid ground. "Are you okay, Jenny?" she asked.

Jenny stood up from her prone position on the ground, brushed herself off, and quite calmly said, "I'm fine. Let's go find that body!"

And so, the four of them started toward the area where they had seen the body on the ground.

The incoming fire raged ahead somewhere in front of them.

CHAPTER ELEVEN

THE BODY AND THE FIRE

"Do you smell that smoke?" Jenny asked. "How close do you suppose that fire is, anyway?"

"Too close for me," Jan quipped back, as she looked to Donnie for comment.

"Not to worry, girls," Donnie told them, as Jenny wondered why Drake was so obviously quiet.

"What do *you* think, Drake?" Jenny asked him.

"I think *any* fire in these parts is *unsafe* and a reason to worry," Drake said, as they forged their way in the direction of where the body they had seen from the gondola earlier that day lay.

Jenny looked worried.

"What makes you say that?" Jenny asked, as the foursome plodded through the grass and the brush.

The Mystery At Lake Tahoe

"For one thing, PG&E, the public utility company in these parts, was determined by the courts to have caused a grand total of thirty-one wildfires. And in the deadly 'Campfire' in Paradise, they were convicted of eighty-four counts of manslaughter!"

"That happens when companies favor profit over human life," Jenny told Drake. "And it doesn't help that PG&E is a public offering company, subject to Wall Street pressures."

"I'm beginning to really like you," Drake told Jenny. "You aren't like other airhead girls I've met vacationing in these parts. You actually have a brain!"

"Jenny's like that," Jan interjected. "I've known her practically all of my life. And she seems to always have her nose in a book! And if her nose isn't in a book, she's usually watching the news or doing research on the internet."

"All work and no play?" Drake asked Jenny.

"If you consider being informed, work," Jenny said. "I guess I'm not much of a fun-time kind of gal."

"I'll say!" Jan said with a giggle.

"I'll take a serious, informed girl over a fun-time kind of gal any day," Drake said, winking at Jenny.

Jenny smiled. She was beginning to like this guy.

"And I like well-informed young men," Jenny told him.

"There you go!" Jan laughed. "Finally! It's a match made in heaven."

And then, Donnie, who was leading the way forward, yelled, "There it is! There's the body!" scaring the feasting vultures away from the now rotting corpse, up into the sky.

Jan and Jenny ran ahead of Donnie and Drake to the body.

"I hate maggots!" was the first thing Jan said. "And the smell isn't too good either!" she added, just as the boys caught up with them.

"What do we do now?" Jenny asked Donnie.

"Well, I do believe we are far enough down the mountain that our cell phones just might work . . . if they've got cell services up and running that is . . ."

"You never know how cell service will be during fires or even winds," Drake interjected. "And it looks like we have both situations here, unfortunately."

"I certainly hope we don't get trapped in the fire," Jenny told him, as Donnie took out his mobile phone and dialed 911.

"Good news!" Donnie proclaimed. "The towers are up and working!"

"That *is* good news!" Jan exclaimed excitedly. "Maybe we can actually get out of here!"

As Donnie explained their situation to the 911 dispatcher, the smell of smoke intensified.

And then Jenny saw the flames!

CHAPTER TWELVE

NO TIME TO RUN

As it turned out, it looked like the flames were moving too fast, and were too close, for the four of them to make a run for it.

Donnie and Drake went immediately into survival mode and told the girls to head for a shallow ditch they saw just feet ahead of them. The girls did as they were told and ran toward the ditch, with Donnie and Drake (carrying the corpse between them) following closely behind Jan and Jenny, watching out for any falling debris from the wind and the fire. The ditch was wide enough and deep enough to offer all of them (including the corpse) protection from the approaching flames.

Donnie pulled two emergency 'fire shelters' made of aluminum foil-woven silica, that firefighters use when trapped in a fire, out of his backpack, and threw one to each of the girls.

The Mystery At Lake Tahoe

"Take these and cover yourselves with these fire shelters when you get into that ditch!" he shouted. "Lay face down and cover yourselves! Hopefully, help is on the way!"

Jenny and Jan were frantic! The winds were gusting, and the approaching flames twirled into the air creating what appeared to be a huge fire tornado!

They did as they were told. Jan and Jenny ran to the ditch, jumped in, lay face down, and covered themselves with the protective fire shields.

Jenny tried to get a signal on her cell phone; however, service was now completely out.

"It's a good thing Donnie got through to 911 earlier," Jenny thought to herself, not wanting to alarm Jan with the terror she felt certain lay ahead for them.

"Jenny, I just want you to know I love you!" Jan told Jenny from under her fire shield. "If this is the end for us, I want you to always know that!" Jan's voice cracked, as she lay there covered and face down in the ditch.

Jenny began to cry, and soon thereafter she began to cough as the smoke from the fire descended upon them.

"Oh, Jan, I love you too!" she screamed. "But we are going to make it out of this. I just know it! Keep the faith, Jan! God has bigger plans in store for us!"

The Mystery At Lake Tahoe

Drake and Donnie quickly joined the girls and readied themselves to jump into the ditch with the girls, with *one* caveat. Donnie pulled *three* fire shields from *his* backpack and *not* just two.

With little or no finesse *or warning,* Donnie and Drake threw the corpse they had carried between them as they ran toward the ditch *into* the ditch, right alongside Jan and Jenny! Then they jumped into the ditch, next to the corpse, turned it face down, and covered it with one of the *three* fire shelter blankets Donnie had pulled from *his* backpack. And then the two boys finally, and at last, covered *themselves* and laid face down in the ditch.

"Try to ignore the stench from our dead friend, girls. We saved the corpse just for you," Donnie said, as they all just lay there, hoping and praying their protective blankets would protect them from the blazing fire now upon them.

Luckily, due to the fact a green, grassy area, surrounded the trench in which they lay, the fire quickly burned past them, and continued its path back up the mountain.

After a few moments of relative quiet, Donnie carefully lifted the protective fire shield from his head and raised himself up in the ditch . . . just enough to assess the situation.

It appeared the prevailing winds had changed the direction of the fire!

Meanwhile, Jenny continued trying to get service on her cell phone as she lay there under the fire shelter, not quite trusting

The Mystery At Lake Tahoe

Donnie's earlier, previous call was sufficient to summon adequate assistance.

Suddenly, Jenny's phone beeped for a few seconds, just long enough for her to send an emergency text.

"I got a signal, guys!' Jenny squealed with excitement. "I do believe we're in luck! Maybe *two* emergency calls will do the trick and will be enough to summon some help!"

"I sure hope so, Jenny!' Donnie told her. "Our little friend here is getting ripe! I can't take much more of this putrid smell!"

"Lest you forget," Jenny quipped in response, "we are *all* stuck *together* in this ditch! It's not pleasant for anyone!"

"I think it's safe for us to get out of this hole, guys!" Drake said interrupting the heady discourse that was beginning once again between Jenny and Donnie. "It appears we aren't in any further danger of fire exposure at this point."

Jan and Jenny lifted their fire shelter blankets, sat upright, and looked around in every direction possible. There was nothing left now of the fire, except for the smell of smoldering ashes and the sight of burned debris.

"Wow! It looks like we've been in a nuclear explosion!" Jan gasped.

And then she stopped short of further comment.

"I think I hear a vehicle approaching!" Jenny exclaimed. "I think they got our distress messages!"

And then, and not before too very long, they were in fact being rescued by the local fire department's overland rescue unit in a four-wheel drive jeep! It was a tight fit, especially with the corpse in tow, but they were on their way back! And most importantly, they were out of imminent danger.

The corpse in the very back of the jeep had not been as lucky.

CHAPTER THIRTEEN

THE SECRETS OF THE DEAD

The two firefighters who showed up to help them were in awe that the foursome even cared to pick up a body that for all intents and purposes should have burned in the fire, along with the four of them. And they were *not* at all shy about expressing that thought.

Jenny, being her confrontational self, told the two firefighters in no uncertain terms that all life was precious and should be treated with utmost respect; and that was exactly what the four of them were trying to do.

"Besides," Jan added, "you do realize that this woman was murdered, and if she was your mother, your sister, or even your neighbor, wouldn't you want to see justice done?"

"How do you know she was murdered? And how do you know this corpse is a woman?"

"When you unwrap the corpse, you will see that it is obviously a woman," Jan told the firefighter, as the jeep bumped along the uneven surface that led them back into town.

"When did you see that?" Jenny whispered.

"I saw it when the boys brought the corpse back to the ditch and wrapped it in the fire shield fabric," Jan whispered back to Jenny. "I know I was supposed to stay wrapped and face down in the ditch, but I peeked anyway. I couldn't help myself."

Jenny smiled. It was so like Jan to look for answers, to leave no proverbial stone unturned, so to speak.

"And how do you know she was murdered?" the same firefighter asked.

"The bullet hole in her forehead will tell you that!" Donnie interjected. "This woman was killed execution style!"

The firefighter who had been interrogating them grew quiet.

"She sure smells bad," the other firefighter said.

"I believe the next stop you make should be the coroner's office," Donnie told the firefighters.

"The body may have secrets to tell," Jan added.

"What secrets could the dead possibly have?" the firefighter who had been questioning them asked.

"For beginners," Drake told him, "the secret of her identity."

The Mystery At Lake Tahoe

"And who knows what other secrets the body may hold," Jenny added, as they bounced along in the crowded vehicle.

And after that, no more was said. And soon they *did* arrive at their first stop, the coroner's office. And the coroner's assistants rushed out of the building to retrieve the body.

As the coroner's crew carefully placed the still wrapped body upon a stretcher and carried it into the coroner's office, Jan looked at Jenny and said, "I really *do wonder* what secrets that body holds."

And Donnie and Drake *knew* that Jan and Jenny would not rest until they found out! After all, they *were* indeed *that* Jan and Jenny!

CHAPTER FOURTEEN

WHO IS SHE?

For a first day of sight-seeing, this one turned out to be a doozy! Jan and Jenny were exhausted, covered in ash, and ready to take a much-needed shower and perhaps even a nap.

Needless to say, Jenny's mom and Aunt Vi were on pins and needles worried about the girls, once they found out there was a forest fire in the area where Jan and Jenny were taking their gondola ride. Of course, once the girls finally were back at the hotel, all was once again getting back to normal. Even though they were anxious to hear about the harrowing experience Jan and Jenny just went through, Jenny's mom and Aunt Vi sensed that the girls were very tired and needed rest before they did or even talked about their day, or anything else. So, they put all of their questions on the back burner and decided to wait for a more convenient time to talk.

The Mystery At Lake Tahoe

Since the coroner had control of the dead female body, all Jan and Jenny could do was to wait patiently for the coroner's results and possibly speculate. Since it was obvious that this was, in fact, a murder that had taken place, an investigation was certain to ensue, and the girls were hopeful the results wouldn't be kept under wraps.

Donnie and Drake went back to their homes as well, to get cleaned up and to await any news that might come from the coroner's office. And since the four of them were considered witnesses, of sorts, having come upon the crime scene, the coroner indicated the authorities would indeed be contacting each of them for a statement.

After Jenny finished her shower, she plopped down on her bed, wet hair wrapped in a towel, put on the hotel provided bathrobe, and began scrolling through her brand-new iPad to see if there were any missing persons notifications in the area that might tell her who the corpse was. Jan, jumped into the shower for her turn with big plans to take a nice, long, restful nap after her shower!

Back in the coroner's examination room, investigation was in progress. The body was opened up for autopsy, and much to the coroner and her staff's amazement and surprise, a computer thumb drive was discovered in the body's intestinal tract! The question then became whether the thumb drive was there intentionally.

"The facts would indicate our Jane Doe more than likely swallowed this, a computer thumb drive, voluntarily," the coroner said, as she removed the device, while making a recorded vocal record of the autopsy in order to properly preserve the trail of evidence relating to the murder. "I surmise this device was swallowed to prevent persons unknown (at this time) from obtaining whatever information is recorded on this device," the coroner added.

The plot was thickening. There was no formal identification on the body, so that factor was still to be determined. And there were also a lot of unanswered questions that needed answering before the case could be closed.

Fingerprints were taken of the deceased, and DNA samples were properly collected. A specialist was called to examine the body for trace evidence, as well as to determine time of death.

One thing was evident. Jane Doe did not go quietly to her death. Defensive wounds on what remained of her decomposing hands and arms told a story of their own.

And as Jenny searched the internet deep into the night, Jan slept, exhausted from their long and frightful day.

CHAPTER FIFTEEN

JANE DOE . . . DAY TWO

It didn't take long to get a fingerprint match and an identity on Jane Doe; because (as it turned out) Jane Doe was an FBI undercover agent named Rosemary Day.

"We'd better call the FBI and get them in on this," the local sheriff informed the coroner. "It would appear we have stumbled into their case."

The coroner agreed.

"Should I make the call, or would you prefer to make the call?" the coroner asked. "What exactly is the protocol here?"

The questions remained unanswered as three, stone-faced FBI agents stormed through the double doors of the coroner's examining room.

"Where's the body?" one of them asked, holding up her badge and identification as an FBI agent.

It was Ms. Wright, an attorney for the FBI and a friend of Jan and Jenny.

"She's right here on the table," the coroner said.

"I have two forensic anthropologist specialists with me who would like to examine the body for both cause of death, as well as for trace evidence that could lead to the apprehension of the murderer." Ms. Wright told the coroner.

The sheriff remained silent as the coroner asked, "But how did you know we had one of your agents?"

"We were just about to call you," the sheriff added.

"We have a tracking device on the now deceased, and we were additionally called," Ms. Wright told the coroner as she put away her identification and badge.

"But who called you?" the sheriff asked.

"That will only be told to you on a 'need to know' basis. And right now, you do not need to know," Ms. Wright staunchly informed the sheriff.

"Before your agents examine the body, they will need to properly suit up," the coroner told Ms. Wright.

"Of course," Ms. Wright told the coroner, who then led the two agent specialists to a decontamination area next to the autopsy room to properly suit up and decontaminate.

The Mystery At Lake Tahoe

"We can't be too careful," the coroner said, once the two agent specialists were properly suited up and decontaminated.

Once the two specialist agents and the coroner returned to the autopsy room where the sheriff had remained guard, and the specialist agents began their examination of the body, the coroner turned to Ms. Wright and said, "I have something to show you. You'd better come with me to my office."

And then the two of them proceeded to the small room with the door placard that said, 'Office of the Coroner', sat down on either side of a desk that was much too large for the room and began to talk, woman to woman.

Ms. Wright began.

"What I am about to tell you, I am telling you in strictest confidence and only to facilitate the processing of this case."

"I'm listening,' the coroner told her. "And then I have something to show you."

"Agent Rosemary was working undercover in a seditionist militia military group that was functioning on the deep web as ACLF, American Constitutional Life Foundation. The moniker was obviously taken in an effort to confuse upstanding Americans that they were dealing with the ACLU, the American Civil Liberties Union. These rapacious individuals were able to defraud mom and pop Americans out of hundreds of millions of dollars through online requests for donations to their cause, which they fraudulently alleged through emails (on the surface web) was to preserve the right of a free America, when the intent was actually to defraud honest Americans into contributing to the acquisition of weaponry and to finance a private army to overthrow the United States of America."

"And so how did the fire figure into this?" the coroner asked, correctly assuming the proximity of the fire had something to do with the execution style killing of undercover Agent Rosemary.

"We have no evidentiary proof as of yet that the two incidents are connected. However, it is our belief the fire was intentionally set and intended to fall on the fault of the local electricity company provider, PG&E, for the express purpose of hiding the cause of the death of undercover Agent Rosemary, presuming (now incorrectly) that an ensuing fire would reach her decomposing body and remove all relevant traces of evidence."

Upon hearing this, the coroner began to open the top drawer of her desk. Ms. Wright drew her gun in response.

"Don't worry," the coroner said. "I'm not going for a gun. I'm going for this," she added as she removed the thumb drive she had found in the stomach of the corpse.

"This was in Agent Rosemary's intestinal track," the coroner told Ms. Wright. "I haven't yet looked at its contents. However, assuming there was no damage to the device, I believe it might be of interest to you."

Ms. Wright smiled, put her gun back under the right-side back of her waistband, and reached out and took the device from the coroner's outstretched hand and said, "We ladies make a fine team!"

The Mystery At Lake Tahoe

CHAPTER SIXTEEN

AND THEN ALONG CAME DOE

The key to the entirety of what was going on with Agent Rosemary, formerly known as Jane Doe, lived and died with Jane Doe. And in her death her remains had a story to tell! And what a story it would turn out to be!

As the forensic anthropologists began assembling the evidence before them, Ms. Wright took a good look at the contents of the thumb drive retrieved from Agent Rosemary's intestines. And what Ms. Wright saw was beyond belief.

That afternoon she met with the girls at the hotel dining room for a late lunch of burgers and fries and strawberry shakes, for which Ms. Wright tried to pay, but was told it was 'on the house', due to Jenny's dad being booked at the hotel with all expenses paid.

The Mystery At Lake Tahoe

"I know I can trust you girls to keep what I am about to tell you in strictest confidence," Ms. Wright began. "And we may need the help of you two sleuths later," she added.

"Besides our statements about the body?" Jenny asked.

"Yes," Ms. Wright replied.

Jan sat wide-eyed trying to keep track of and understand everything Ms. Wright was saying, as Ms. Wright proceeded.

The thumb drive shows and proves according to the evidence contained therein . . ." she began . . .

"Could you please not speak in legal talk?" Jan interrupted. "I'd like to understand what you are saying."

"Sorry," Ms. Wright told Jan. "I'll try to keep this as simple as possible."

Jenny smiled.

"Put in the simplest terms, there are three levels of the internet. There's the dark web content that exists on darknets. This level of the internet requires specific software configuration. The dark web is used for illegal activity and may also be used by journalists and activists. The point is that it is not generally accessible by regular folks. The deep web may be considered part of the dark web, but the basic difference is the deep web can be accessed (reached) through normal search engines with a username and password. The level normal, regular people like you two girls use is the surface net. And that's accessed through so-called carriers of public information accessible to all, such as Google and Yahoo."

"And?" Jan asked, trying to take in everything Ms. Wright was telling her.

"And the culprits who killed Agent Rosemary used all three levels of the net in order to carry out a nefarious and illegal enterprise. They hacked the deep web to steal names, addresses, phone numbers, and email addresses of unsuspecting individuals; and then they used the dark web to enter into drug deals (and worse) to further finance illegal activities, believing they couldn't be found there. They also *posed* as a legal nonprofit corporation, calling themselves the 'American Constitutional Life Foundation', ACLF, and encouraged millions, through internet emails, to contribute to what people thought was a noble cause."

"That name and the initials sound suspiciously similar to the 'American Civil Liberties Union', the ACLU," Jenny interjected.

"Precisely! But that's not the half of it," Ms. Wright continued, after taking a short pause to take a long sip of her strawberry shake. "The point *is* that this is just *one* of a series of undercover militia groups intending to take over our democracy and turn it into an autocracy, a system of government intended to be run by one person with absolute power."

"Is that what January 6, 2022 was all about?" Jan asked.

"To be frank, yes," Ms. Wright told the girls.

The Mystery At Lake Tahoe

"Tell us what we can do!" Jan exclaimed, with great concern in her voice.

"I would like you two girls to go undercover on all three areas of the internet and see what you can find to confirm what I have been telling you."

"Is it dangerous?" Jenny asked.

"I hope not. And I don't believe so, as you will go through a blind, well-protected server."

Jan scratched her head, uncertain of how she should respond.

"I'm all in!" Jenny exclaimed, much to Jan's great surprise.

And then, after thinking for only a moment, Jan exclaimed, "Me too! It's all for one and one for all! And I know two more guys who will help us!"

"Donnie and Drake?" Ms. Wright asked.

"Yes! How did you know?" Jenny asked.

"We at the FBI know just about everything," Ms. Wright said with a smile. "And besides, we talked to them already; and they agreed to help as well."

"But why us?" Jenny asked out of pure curiosity.

"You four found the body, and so it's logical. And besides, you can do this incognito as you're just a bunch of kids who are innocent and beyond suspicion."

Jan and Jenny nodded their heads as Ms. Wright further added, "Oh, and I cleared this already with your parents."

The Mystery At Lake Tahoe

"What did they say?" Jan and Jenny asked in unison.

"Both sets of parents said something to the effect that they hoped sitting at a computer would keep you out of physical trouble."

Jan and Jenny laughed.

"And tomorrow you are scheduled at 11:00 AM to make your formal statements," Ms. Wright added.

"Will Donnie and Drake be there?" Jan asked.

"Of course," Ms. Wright told them. "And I'll be right there too!"

Jan and Jenny smiled. It would be good to see the boys.

"Do you have any questions?" Ms. Wright asked.

"Not really," Jan said, "except that . . . will we be going out to lunch after that?"

"Of course," Ms. Wright told Jan with a smile. "It's the least we can do to preserve the course of democracy."

And then Ms. Wright told them the story of her maternal grandparents who were taken in the holocaust and died at Auschwitz in one of the forty concentration camps operated by Nazi, Germany in Poland during World War II and the Holocaust.

And that served to further the determination of the girls that they should never allow *that* to happen again.

Tears ran down Jan's cheeks. She knew that this time even more than a mystery needed solving.

CHAPTER SEVENTEEN

DINNER, BED & STATEMENTS

After their confidential meeting with Ms. Wright, it was nearly time for the dinner luau at the hotel, and then (of course) it would be straight to bed for Jan and Jenny! Jan wondered how in the world, after only *two days* of their Lake Tahoe trip, they had managed to stumble into such an elaborate scheme to *basically* take over the world . . . or at least to take over America! And *now*, they were going to be a part of helping to bring the bad guys to justice? How could this be happening?

As the two of them walked back to the hotel to join Jenny's family for the luau dinner, Jan lowered her head in dismay.

"While it all sounds *very* exciting to help the FBI again with Ms. Wright, I *was* hoping we could enjoy Lake Tahoe and all its beauty on this trip, and *maybe* just relax for a change, Jenny."

The Mystery At Lake Tahoe

"Oh, Jan," Jenny began, "this is exactly what we do! This is how we save the world! If we don't help *this time*, there may not be an America, or even a world, as we know it! We may not even have the privilege *or* the freedom to enjoy the beauty of what this country of ours and the *world* has to offer! Don't you *see?* There are people out there *right now* plotting to take our freedom away from us! We *can't* let that happen. And don't worry, Jan. This is a three week stay! I am sure there will be time left when we are finished helping with all of this to do *everything* we want to do!"

"All I really *want* to do at this point is to just *relax,*" Jan very uncharacteristically told Jenny.

(It was Jenny who was usually the hesitant one.)

Jan was exhausted. What they had come upon *this* time was almost too much for her to comprehend.

I guess you're right, of course" Jan finally said, after pausing to think for a moment, and then quickly acquiescing to Jenny's cause and effect' explanation and the responsibility thrown at them to save democracy from what appeared to her to be a total destruction of America. "I really *do* understand," she told Jenny. "It's just so mind boggling to me. I really thought America was a safe place! Now I'm finding out that no one is safe anymore! How could this *ever* happen?"

Jenny patted Jan on the back to reassure her.

"No worries, my friend," she said. "All will be well, because 'all's well that ends well', as they say! And *please* do not ask me who *they* are like my dad does!" Jenny added with a laugh. "Now, let's go get dressed in the Hawaiian shirts my mom bought for us to wear at the luau, and let's go and eat some yummy luau food!"

(Jan had forgotten all about the luau during all of the excitement.)

"I do believe that's the best idea you've had all day!" she told Jenny. "I had actually *forgotten* all about the luau!"

Shortly thereafter, the girls arrived back at the hotel *intending* to go *straight* to their bedroom in the suite to put on the Hawaiian shirts Jenny's mom had carefully hung on hangers in the closet for them to wear. However, when they exited the private elevator that brought them to the suite, there stood Aunt Vi and Jenny's mom, dressed in their Hawaiian garb, patiently waiting for the girls to explain everything that had happened *that* day as well as what had happened the *previous* day, a tale Jan and Jenny had not yet told!

Jan rolled her eyes and sighed, exasperated at the thought of having to go through all of what had happened in her mind once again. She realized they deserved an explanation, even if it had to be a limited one due to the promises of confidentiality she and Jenny had made. So, that's exactly what they did. Jenny grabbed some drinks from the refrigerator, and Jan directed them to the outside balcony veranda, in order that the four of them could sit comfortably as the somewhat limited recap of the two days unfolded.

After the somewhat timely, although limited explanation, the four of them were famished; and so (after the girls were dressed in their Hawaiian shirts for the occasion) they took the elevator down to the party area to join the rest of the family, where the Hawaiian festivities were almost in full swing, Jenny's dad on stage playing his trumpet with the band, as a pig wrapped in palm leaves roasted in a Hawaiian style barbeque that had been pit dug right outside, not yet ready to be ceremoniously carried Hawaiian style into the room.

Tomorrow they would go to the authorities and give their official statements.

Jenny's mom and her Aunt Vi took what they had been told in stride; and even though they were frightened for the girls, they felt confident Ms. Wright would keep the girls safe. However, only time would tell; and time, just like the body in the morgue, still had many secrets to reveal.

CHAPTER EIGHTEEN

THE SECRETS OF THE DEAD

Jan and Jenny were up bright and early the next morning. They showered and dressed, and after eating heartily of the room service breakfast Jenny's dad had ordered for the entire family, the dishes were set aside; and Jan and Jenny went to their room to ready themselves mentally for the statements they were about to give.

"I don't know why I'm so nervous," Jenny told Jan. "All we have to do is tell the truth about what we saw."

"But where should we begin?" Jan asked.

"I think we begin at the beginning," Jenny said. "Where else could we possibly begin?" Jenny added.

Jan smiled.

"I only wish I could relax, Jenny."

"So do I, Jan!" Jenny replied. "Maybe, just maybe *someday* we'll be able to really do that."

"I hope so, Jenny," Jan said, shaking her head in disbelief.

"But this is bigger than just the two of us, so we just have to be strong, Jan."

"I'm scared, Jenny. I've never felt like this before, and I don't understand all of it, even though I know I need to help."

"I think this is just a part of our growing up, Jan," Jenny told her. "And maybe this is all just a part of who we are."

"You keep saying that, Jenny. And I agree, but I've never felt this afraid of things during any of our past adventures. The thought of crazy people wanting to overthrow our government and our way of life just makes me sick! What are they thinking?"

"I don't know, Jan. Maybe they think they will garner some kind of favor in their planned takeover. Maybe they think they will be elevated in society in some way. I just don't know."

"Maybe they are all being manipulated, and then they are simply manipulating others with their lies and their hate. They do carry a lot of hate with them, Jenny. Don't they understand we are a melting pot, and America is a grand and great experiment?"

"I don't think so, Jan. I think some of them are still fighting the civil war. And then all of the big oil companies are churning for wealth, right along with Wall Street; and people feel like they should have more . . . more than they need . . . and more than they deserve.

And all of this noise (because that is all it is) and all of the lies appeal to them; because it gives them an excuse for their sad and sorry lives."

"Did you think of that all by yourself?" Jan asked, as she grabbed her purse.

"Well, not exactly, Jan. Me and my Dad have these long talks sometimes, and he tells me stuff," Jenny told Jan, grabbing her purse as well, as the two of them headed for the private elevator.

"Going down!" Jenny announced.

"Try to stay safe!" Jenny's mom yelled.

"Don't take any wooden nickels," Jenny's brother, John, told the girls as the elevator door closed.

"It's not fair! Those two have all of the fun!" Christine complained, as Jenny's Aunt Vi shook her head.

"Hopefully, you'll never have *that* kind of fun," Jenny's Aunt Vi told Christine, knowingly.

And then the girls were off and running (so to speak) and right on time, at 11:00 AM they were sitting at the sheriff's office, adjacent to the coroner's office, in the lobby with Donnie and Drake, ready to give their official statements for the record.

However, as Donnie entered the interrogation room first, to give his statement, Ms. Wright appeared at the door and motioned to the girls for them to follow her.

The girls smiled at Drake and followed Ms. Wright.

The Mystery At Lake Tahoe

"I'm sure we'll be back shortly," Jan said. "Ms. Wright promised to take the four of us to lunch!"

And then Jan and Jenny went with Ms. Wright to another room where they were given even more detail that Jan (for one) really did not want to know.

"It appears that before Agent Rosemary's final demise, being shot in the head, she was violently beaten and taken sexual advantage of several times, by more than one individual. She fought back. And because she fought back, we were able to collect DNA from three individuals, from the sexual attacks and from under her fingernails."

Jan and Jenny's eyes widened.

"How awful!" Jenny said.

"And additionally," Ms. Wright continued, ignoring the brief interruption, "we were able to run the samples through a criminal database and identify the three culprits. The bullet in her forehead, intended to look like a mob hit execution, also gave us evidence. That evidence, and the bullet striations, was matched to a gun from a previous murder, that was thought to be carefully stored in evidence, but is now missing."

Jan gasped.

"Do you mean to tell me a bunch of criminals are trying to overthrow the United States of America?" Jan asked.

"As ludicrous as it sounds, that is exactly what I am saying," Ms. Wright told the girls.

The Mystery At Lake Tahoe

"But who are they?" Jenny asked.

"They are nobodies," Ms. Wright told the girls. "They are nobodies trying to get attention from history by siding with a bunch of wealthy reprobates who want more than they need and much more than they deserve. They believe they will be pardoned for all their sins after the takeover of this country."

But how do you know this?" Jenny asked.

"We have our identifications, and we are in pursuit of them as I speak," Ms. Wright said, frankly answering Jenny's question.

"Are we in danger?" Jan asked.

"Yes. I won't kid you girls. It is our belief that one or more of the culprits observed the four of you teens at the site through remote drone surveillance."

"How do you know that?" Jan asked.

"They posted everything on their dark web site," Ms. Wright explained.

"And so, what happens next?" Jenny asked.

"The four of you will be put under protective custody," Ms. Wright told the girls. "But there is a twist."

"A twist?" Jenny asked. "What's the twist?"

"What is good for the goose is good for the gander," Ms. Wright explained. "Your protective custody will be in plain sight and posted on the web everywhere."

"As a trap?" Jan asked.

The Mystery At Lake Tahoe

"Yes. You four will be the bait, but you will be bait with a difference. You see, we know who those men are; and so, the minute they appear anywhere where you are, they will be arrested. In the meantime, the four of you will be hailed as heroes, having found the body leading to evidence of a country-wide takeover. The boys have already been informed, and so has your dad and Jan's family," Ms. Wright explained.

"And my mom and my Aunt Vi? Jenny asked.

"Your dad wanted to explain it to your aunt and mother," Ms. Wright told her. "He felt they would be more comfortable that way."

"Then we don't have to go into hiding?" Jan asked.

"For all intents and purposes, you will be relaxing and just be having fun," Ms. Wright told the girls. "And the boys will be posing as waiters at the hotel and put up in a room there as well."

"Well, I do like the idea of fun," Jan told Ms. Wright. "I just don't like the idea of being sitting ducks!"

Jenny smiled.

"Don't you get it, Jan?" Jenny asked Jan. "The four of us were sitting ducks the minute we helped retrieve that body! At least now we will be having some fun as *protected* sitting ducks!"

"I guess that has to be okay," Jan finally said. "I do like fun!"

And then the girls left to give their official statements, and once all four statements were signed, sealed and delivered, Ms.

Wright took the foursome to lunch as promised; and it was a most fabulous lunch!

They didn't even notice the protective custody had started or that they were being recorded. They might only be helping to melt the tip of an iceberg; however, the iceberg was huge, and thus seemed better to both Jan and Jenny than sitting at a computer uncovering a plot.

And when questioned as to why the plan had suddenly changed, Ms. Wright simply told the four of them, "We have experts for that; and besides, the dead *do* reveal their secrets!"

And that was exactly how it was!

The Mystery At Lake Tahoe

CHAPTER NINETEEN

LET'S HAVE SOME FUN!

After their lunch and meeting with Ms. Wright, Jan and Jenny decided to go poolside and get some sun with the boys, while the four of them planned what fun activity would be next. After all, that was the plan, so to speak . . . to be sitting ducks!

Jan scrolled down her iPad, as they sat poolside in the lounge chairs, checking out all of the great summer fun to be had at the lake.

"What are you in the mood to do, Jenny?" Jan asked, with little true enthusiasm; because they *were*, after all, sitting ducks!

"Wow, Jan," Jenny replied. "With *that* tone of voice, how am I supposed to get excited about doing anything? Lighten up, girl!"

Jan laughed, realizing *at once* that *for once* Jenny was right. So, she started reading off the list of things to do aloud to Jenny, trying to pique Jenny's curiosity, as she attempted to garner up her *own* enthusiasm.

"Now, this sounds like it's right up your alley, the small group photography scenic half-day tour. How does that sound?"

"Keep on reading down that list," Jenny said. "That's a little too long for us to be 'sitting ducks', I think."

The boys said nothing; and when the poolside waiter came by, they ordered sodas all around.

"We might as well live it up since everything is on the house!" Donnie laughed.

"Keep laughing, laughing boy," Jenny smirked. "Because when evening falls, you two boys will be pretending you are waiters, 'sitting duck' waiters!"

Donnie stopped laughing as Jan continued.

"Well, we are way too young for the wine country tour," Jan surmised, tongue in cheek.

The girls laughed, and the boys just stared out at the pool wondering why they weren't in on the decision about what they would do next, since they *were* (after all) all four of them, sitting ducks!

Jan continued reading off their choices aloud so that all four of them could hear.

The Mystery At Lake Tahoe

"Hmmm. This sounds interesting! How about the electric bike tour of the east shore trail? It's less exhausting than going on our own pedal power, at least."

After thinking for a moment, Jenny replied, "Keep that one marked. That sounds easy enough. What else do you have?"

"Oh, here's a goody! There's a charter sailboat cruise that sails out of Emerald Bay! It's a two-hour sail, on a "Keep Tahoe Blue", forty-foot sailboat, that uses wind power for an eco-friendly voyage without the smell and noise of gas-powered motors!"

"Now you're speaking my language, Jan! Let's check that out!" Jenny told her.

The boys agreed it would be a *perfect* outing, realizing four sitting ducks in a sailboat would be nothing less than poetic justice.

"It looks pretty cool; and it won't take up a whole lot of time," Jan said. "Yes, let's check into this for sure!"

And so, the four of them paid a visit to the concierge, hoping they would have enough pull to get the four of them on the charter sailboat the next day for that two-hour tour.

To their great surprise, the arrangements were easily made, even though they were *very* last minute *and* off the cuff, so to speak.

"You'll be leaving at noon, tomorrow," the concierge said, handing each of them their ticketed passage for the Emerald Lake sailboat tour.

The Mystery At Lake Tahoe

What they didn't know was that two undercover agents would also be joining them for the trip, one to captain the sailboat, and one to be the captain's first mate. And *those* arrangements were made shortly *after* the four of them departed the concierge desk.

The Mystery At Lake Tahoe

CHAPTER TWENTY

NIGHT AND DAY!

That night the boys played the parts of two dutiful waiters, waiting on the dinner hotel guests hand and foot, as Jan and Jenny readied themselves to meet them after their evening shift to go dancing in the main room where Jenny's dad and his band were the main attraction. Jenny's mom and Aunt Vi remained in the penthouse watching movies with John and Christine, as the four of *them* stuffed their faces with buttered popcorn and drank cold sodas.

"Have a good time with the boys," Jenny's mom told the two girls, as they hopped on the private elevator that would take them down to the lobby.

Everything the girls and Donnie and Drake happened to be doing was covered by surveillance. And so far, as far as Ms. Wright was concerned, everything was going exactly and precisely according to plan.

And so, the four of them played it as though everything was normal. They went dancing to the music of Jenny's dad's band until the wee hours of the morning, drank lots of soda and never went to the bathroom alone. In fact, Jenny hoped surveillance ended at the bathroom stall, but (of course) nothing was for certain; and so she tried to be as modest as possible. (And as to that, Jan just laughed.)

After the music ended, the girls said good night to the boys and took the private elevator back up to the penthouse suite, while Jenny's dad packed up his music and trumpet and the band broke down the music stands and chairs for storage.

As the girls entered the suite, Jenny said, "Having fun isn't as easy as it seems. I'm really tired!"

And as to that, Jan completely agreed.

And then, as the girls walked toward the kitchen area of the suite, they noticed Jenny's mother had a guest. It was Ms. Wright! Jenny's brother and sister and her Aunt Vi were fast asleep.

"Since you two girls are obviously out and about as required of you," Ms. Wright began, "I have something to give you."

Jan and Jenny stopped right in their tracks and looked at Ms. Wright in astonishment. What could she possibly want to be giving them?

And then Ms. Wright handed each of them a watch.

The Mystery At Lake Tahoe

"These are trackers. Put them on your wrists and do not take them off until this thing is all over and done," she said.

Jenny's mother laughed.

"You're getting Dick Tracy watches," she said.

Jan and Jenny were dumfounded.

"What are Dick Tracy watches?" Jenny asked.

"Never mind," Jenny's mother told her. "It was a comic strip that was in the Sunday funny papers long before your time."

As the girls looked on bewildered, Ms. Wright told them, "I know you don't know who Dick Tracy is, but think of these watches as communication devices out of the future."

"Oh, like on the TV show, Star Trek?" Jan asked.

"Exactly," Ms. Wright replied. And just like on Star Trek, the watches are also communicators you can use if and when you get into any trouble. And since they are tracking devices that are small and inconspicuous, they are unlikely to be noticed. And the button on the top of the LED read out only has to be pushed to summon help."

"Anything else?" Jenny asked.

"I should also tell you everything you say and everything anyone says to you will be recorded," Ms. Wright told the girls. "And the boys have these too. They're being outfitted right now."

"I guess you girls better be careful about what you say," Jenny's mom told them. "Big brother is watching you."

Jenny laughed. This time she recognized the reference.

"It's from that book we had to read in school, 1984!" she told Jan, who was already familiar with the reference.

"I know. We were in the same English class, remember?"

Ms. Wright shook her head.

"Now, I know how brave you two girls are; and I want to tell you right now to not take any chances. Tonight, we began setting the trap. Your activities were recorded and posted on the dark web where the FBI heralded you four kids as heroes for finding the body of our fallen agent in arms, Rosemary. And now, we expect that the snakes in the grass will raise their evil heads and strike at any time."

The girls' eyes widened.

"Don't worry," Ms. Wright told them. "We have your backs."

And then Jenny's mother advised the girls to shower and to get right into bed and to get plenty of sleep.

"You girls have a big day ahead of you," she said.

And if the truth was to be told, this was most certainly not the kind of vacation the girls had hoped it would be. However, it was what it was, and now they had to play the hand that was dealt to them.

The Mystery At Lake Tahoe

CHAPTER TWENTY-ONE

EMERALD BAY

A new day dawned. Jan and Jenny dressed in their sailing garb, not forgetting to put on the tracking watches provided by Ms. Wright. The boys met them in the lobby at 11:45 AM sharp, so they could arrive at the boat by high noon. Jenny decided to bring her camera and camera gear with her, because the concierge said there would be great photographic opportunities from the water on Emerald Bay.

Donnie and Drake walked the girls out to the waiting minivan that was provided by the hotel free of charge, again, because Jenny's dad was the star performer at the hotel. The foursome exited the double front doors of the hotel and piled into the minivan.

Do either of you boys have any sailing experience?" Jenny timidly asked.

"My dad took me sailing a couple times. I know a little bit about sailing," Drake told her.

Hearing that, Jenny seemed relieved. At least someone knew something about sailing! Now, it wasn't as though she didn't *trust* the boat captain, but since they *were* 'sitting ducks' on a sting operation, it couldn't hurt to have back-up . . . just in case.

"That's great!" Jenny told Drake. "It will be good to have an extra hand on board! Jan and I don't know much about sailing, but we're fast learners!"

"As long as Jenny doesn't get seasick," Jan interjected with a laugh.

"I took Dramamine before we left, just in case," Jenny added. "So, I'm raring to go! Besides, I only got seasick once when I was sailing, and I really do love the water."

Drake smiled. Jenny was a real trooper. He liked that about Jenny.

It was just a short trip to Emerald Bay; so, before they knew it, they were there, staring at the awesome chartered sailboat they were about to board.

The captain of the forty-foot sailboat (who was actually an undercover FBI agent on the job) greeted them as they walked up to the dock to board.

"Welcome aboard, mates! Are you ready for a fantastic tour of Emerald Bay?" he asked.

The Mystery At Lake Tahoe

"Yes!" they all answered in unison, as Jan and Jenny looked around, checking to see if anything "seemed suspicious.

"So far, so good," Jan whispered to Jenny, as they went aboard the sailboat and took their seats.

As they all finished putting on and securely fastening the life jackets they were handed as they boarded the sailboat, the captain and his first mate set the sails; and they slowly took off on a smooth ride, traveling down picturesque Emerald Bay. Jenny grabbed her camera and took several shots of the bay from different angles. A flock of geese flew overhead, and Jenny captured the shot beautifully! The captain began his informative narrative, describing points of interest as they continued sailing down the lake.

The lake was very quiet for that particular time of day. To Jan, that seemed unusual, since it was the beginning of summer at Lake Tahoe. She imagined there would be a lot more activity on the water.

"Where is everybody?" Jan asked the captain. "I thought it was crowded out here in summertime?"

The captain cleared his throat, as if he was nervous, and he answered, "Good observation, little lady. Yes, you are correct. It is unusually quiet today, indeed."

And *then* Jan turned and saw a motorboat fast approaching them.

"Hey, guys," she said, to Jenny, Donnie, and Drake, "I think something *may* be going on here."

They were *all* wondering, at that point, what the motorboat was doing. It was coming a little too close to them for comfort! And it looked like it was about to crash into the side of the sailboat!

Jenny started taking multiple photographs of the approaching motorboat, when the captain said, "Good work, Jenny."

Jenny looked at Jan, bewildered. Jan shrugged her shoulders as if confused. Donnie and Drake didn't know what to do, because the captain brandished a side weapon. And he and his first mate, who had been working the sails, walked to the side of the boat.

"What's happening?" Jan and Jenny asked in unison.

"We're undercover agents, and we're here to protect you," the man posing as the ship's captain said. All boat trips on this lake were canceled for today, except for this boat trip; so, the approaching motorboat that you see now is highly suspect, and you four could be in danger. Please immediately go below deck."

And then the foursome did as they were told.

CHAPTER TWENTY-TWO

IT'S ALL OVER!

Even though it was quite comfortable below deck, the foursome found it impossible to relax. How could they relax, anyway? Now they were 'sitting ducks' sitting below deck, all except for Jan (that is) who began to immediately pace back and forth in the small below deck space intended for sleeping.

"This is a very nice sailboat," Jenny said, attempting to lighten the mood.

Her words were of no help.

Suddenly, shots rang out from above deck; and Jenny was the first to push the button on her watch, followed by the others!

"I see you two have 007 watches, too!" Donnie exclaimed. "Let's hope they work!"

And work they did! Shortly thereafter, the whirling sound of helicopter blades could be heard.

The Mystery At Lake Tahoe

"It's a trap!" one of the three men in the motorboat shouted.

The first mate brought a megaphone from a storage box and handed it to the captain.

"You're surrounded by agents of the FBI!" the captain shouted. "Your only chance of survival is to surrender!"

"Or we can ram your little sailboat and sink you as we die! We can all die together!"

"These guys are insane," the captain whispered to the first mate. "I could shoot them all right from here! But our orders are to take them alive, so that is not our first option."

"You could wing them," the first mate told the captain.

"That's an idea," the captain replied, as he raised his Glock .40 S&W pistol and readied his shot.

"Not a good idea!" the man on the motorboat shouted. "We have explosives onboard, and we're ready to detonate."

"All the better to shoot you!" the captain shouted, as his first mate unholstered *his* Glock .40 S&W pistol and also readied to shoot.

Both were sharp shooters and quickly disabled, but did not kill, the three men for whom they had set this trap.

As the three evil snakes screamed and writhed on the deck of their small motorboat, no detonation occurred. The threat of detonation was a bluff, a lie, just like all the other lies they'd helped to spread from the dark web onto the internet. In this instance the best laid plans were the plans the FBI had laid!

The four teens below the deck heard the sounds of multiple motorboats approaching. It was the good guys! The three wounded men were arrested. Their motorboat was towed to shore. Their phones, laptops and whatever other electronic devices and equipment they had on board their motorboat was quickly confiscated. One of the boats that had heretofore surrounded them took them to shore.

"Evil won't raise it's head today," the captain told his first mate. "And now, it is time to finish this tour!" he said. "Call the kids up here!"

And so, it was done! All was safe! The tour was completed. And the boys didn't have to play waiters anymore. They would be debriefed; but for the remainder of those three weeks, there would be nothing but fun and relaxation for Jan and Jenny!

"All I can say," Jenny sighed, as they went back up on deck, "is I'm sure glad we all were wearing lifejackets!"

And then they all laughed, including the captain and the first mate! The sky was blue! They were no longer sitting ducks! They were just four kids out to have a good time!

And that was even if Jan and Jenny were *that* Jan and Jenny!

"And the bittersweet mystery of life Continues..."